Mirror to the Teenage Soul

By Amanda McFadden and Trent McFadden

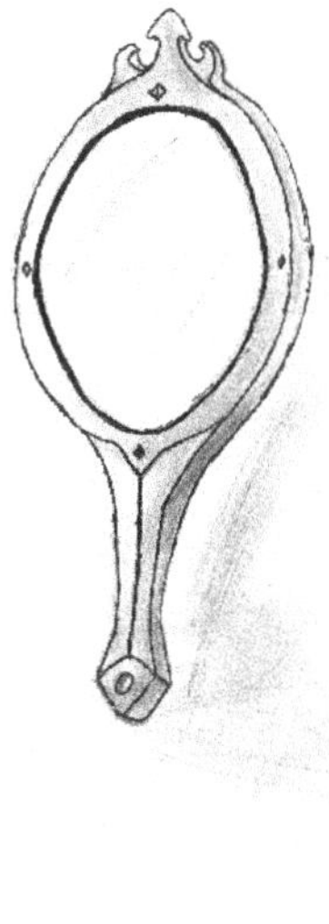

First Edition, October 2024

ISBN: 979-8-330-37414-4

Publisher: IngramSpark
www.ingramspark.com

For any inquiries regarding this book, please contact the author at
www.amandamcfadden.com

To William, Trevor, Samantha, and all our family. We would never have done this without you. Most importantly, we thank God for giving us this chance.

Table of Contents

Introduction

This collection was a long-time coming, but like adolescence, it has taken some twists and turns along the way. This is now a collaborative effort with my teenage son, Trent.

The collection is split into two main sections: *Then...* (my poetry) and *Now...* (his poetry). Please expect a lot of ill-informed, sappy, love poems along with beyond-your-years insightful prose.

Some of these poems were inspired by real events, some are pure fiction, some are satire, and some are a mixture—but they are all for your reading pleasure.

To start off, I have included the cornerstone of my collection, "The Sorrowful," on the following page. It is the first poem I shared in a high school literature and art publication. It is also the poem that made me want to hone and sharpen my craft.

The Sorrowful

With every human's breath
draws the breath of hope

With every human's heart
beats the beat of love

With every human's mind
thinks the thought of life

All except the sorrowful
for they no longer hope, love, or live

Then…

Complicated Love

When you are young, romantic love is a brand-new adventure. Every crush is “the one” and every heartbreak is earth shattering.

Always & Forever

Touch me
Touch me until I melt away

Hold me
Hold me tighter than ever

Kiss me
Kiss me until I turn to flames

Tell me
Tell me that you love me

Love me
Love me always and forever

A Death in the Heart

Have you ever had a death in the heart?
The kind that comes without warning?

Have you ever had a death in the heart?
The kind that washes over your soul with mourning?

Have you ever had a death in the heart?
The kind that happens on an ordinary day like this?

Have you ever had a death in the heart?
The kind that causes you much pain and removes all bliss?

Have you ever had a death in the heart?
The kind that turns your whole heart black?

Have you ever had a death in the heart?
The kind that changes your life and you can't go back

Don't Leave Me

Don't leave me.

For years, I loved one man
For years, my heart was not free
For years, I was his number one fan

For years, I knew him
Or at least I thought I did
For years, my love grew dim
But still, this, I hid

For years, I was hurt by this deceit
Yet, I kept my love strong
For years, I thought we were complete
Why didn't I see I was wrong?

Then I found you
And you kept me entertained
Now I can say what is true
From you, it is love I have obtained

Don't leave me.

Falling for You

Whenever we part
There is a tug at my heart

Your love is what I long for
You've mended the heart he tore

Wherever we are, whatever we do
I just love to be with you

In the beginning, I fought it
I tried to cover with wit

I hope this doesn't make you sad
But I'm falling for you bad

Guilty Lust

Guilt lies where my heart once was
The pain of knowing my own sinful lust
overtakes my soul with shame
I took for granted our unspoken trust

Foolishly acted upon his pull on me
The wind of my passion was but a gust
that opened a door and brought in pain
Which I tried to wipe away like dust

The burning kisses that set me on fire
and filled my heart with disgust
Giving into this powerful lure
Thinking this was not a need but a must

Forgetting the comforts of love
and holding close the excitement of lust

How

How I could love such a brute of a man
How he could hold my soul in his hand

How he could hurt me once, twice, and more
How I could know there was more hurt in store

How I could faithfully hope for a life with him
How he could alter my life in just a whim

How he could tell me of their combined passion
How I could listen in friendly fashion

I Still Love You

I still love you
I know it has been a while
But every time I see your beautiful face
I break into a smile

There is a pain in my heart every time I pass you
I know I am seeing someone new
But there is one thing—
He is not you

He will fade like winter to spring
All I am trying to say is
I still love you

Love

The emotion we all feel
Deep down in our hearts
The hungry heart's meal
Many seas, it parts

Its power is wondrous
The satisfaction is great
The uses are numerous
Its arrival is never late

What can do all this?
Why, love's first kiss!

Love Is

Love is a virus without a cure
and I am sick

Love is a cat without a purr
and I am silent

Love is a door without a key
and I am trapped

Love is a flower without pollen
and I am incomplete

Love is a room without a floor
and I am empty

Love is tiger without a roar
and I am gentle

Love is within me without a doubt

Love Survivor

The commitment of love held sacred to me...

As I looked my tempter in the face
I kept my love locked deep inside
No matter how much my heart would race
I just let the emotions subside

My faith in love, even stronger than life
A silent promise when I began to love
I became not a friend but a wife
I thought we fit like hand in glove

But now I see you wearing a mitten
I see her tug on your skin
With one look I see she was bitten
By the virus known as lover's sin

My heart flooded with tears
Too numerous to count
Sobbing in a place that no one hears
And pain for no account

On the outside my eyes are dry
My heart so torn and shattered
That I cannot even cry
My soul so worn and battered

Yet love is still sacred to me

Loving You

My heart you broke
You treated my love as a joke

You are with her
And my world's a blur

How could you do this
To our rightful bliss?

The touch I still hold
That's warmth has gone cold

Forgive you? I will not
Sorrow is all you brought

With this anger I could kill
But love you? I do still

My Dream Guy

(satire)

I met my dream guy at the mall
That is where he gave me his number to call

He was not the usual tall, dark, and handsome kind
I could see in his eyes he had something on his mind

His hair was straggly, and his ears stuck out
But unlike other guys, he did not cuss and shout

He was gentle and kind
You could say he was quite a find

A week later I called his number
But on the other end was the local plumber

My Love

The love of my life is most special
The sight of him, to my heart, is beneficial

His voice, I know like no other tone
I would protect his life over my own

His laugh sends warmth and love to my heart
Leaving an imprint long after we part

Only we know of the love we share
A love not felt by many a pair

Two Faces

They circle each other
In the light and dark

Never quite aligning
Each leaving a separate mark

Both are equally appealing
My heart torn between
My past and my present
With my future unseen

I must decide only one
How can I choose?
How do I pick?
Which one will I lose?

Two Loves

With numerous examples
I can explain my love for them
Living off the same source of love
As two flowers with one stem

Shining differently in the sun
As a multi-faceted precious stone
Looking open and inviting
As a sky with a pinkish tone

Such complicated emotions
Yet none of these analogies suffice
Whether meek or strong
You will, in time, pay the price

For one, friendship was the end
I spent five years loving him
And now there is a bright light
So, my love began to grow dim

Compassion, politeness, intelligence
A man with the qualities I admire
The ability to make me laugh
And the flame that burns the fire

With the help of no analogy or comparison
Now I must choose a man
And the real question is not if I will
But if I can.

Why Do I Still Love You?

I cry myself to sleep at night
Thinking of our happy times
Knowing you did not do me right
I feel my heart is not worth two dimes

I try to stop these feelings inside
Because you are the one I blame
I feel as though I have died
When my love for you has no flame

I try to remember you as you were
But those memories seem to fade
I see you dancing with her
And the mess my love has made

I tell myself never again
You shall be the last man I trust
I know there are other men
But you are the bread, and they are the crust

Why Don't You Look at Me?

Why don't you look at me?
Did I do something wrong?

Why don't you look at me?
Don't you love me?

Why don't you look at me?
Am I too ugly?

Why don't you look at me?
Do you doubt my love?

Why don't you look at me?
Is there someone else?

Why don't you look at me?
Did I forget something?

Why don't you answer me?

With You

With you, I am a bird
And your voice is the wind

With you, I am an Olympian
And your love is my medal

With you, I am an explorer
And your heart is my terrain

With you, I am anything
And your love is mine

Unrequited Love

Nothing is more gut-wrenching than loving someone who does not feel the same.

Crushed by A Crush

I had a crush on you.
This is true.

I thought you returned my emotion.
But you are your only devotion.

I saw you for your pretty face.
Through a veil of lace.

Seeing not your soul but everything above.
I tried every way to show you my love.

One day, I saw a gleam in your eye.
I thought—he wants to be my guy.

But when you brushed away your curl,
I saw it was for another girl.

I know I should have known better,
When I saw her pass you a love letter.

All my dreams shattered like glass,
When I saw you with this other lass.

I've learned to let it go.
But you're no longer my love, you're my foe.

For A Moment

For a moment...
we embraced.

For a moment...
my heart raced.

For a moment...
he cared.

For a moment...
my love was shared.

For a moment...
we were one.

For a moment...
our love shone like a sun.

For a moment...
he loved me.

For a moment...
my dream was reality.

Forbidden Love

Your bright blond hair puts the sun to shame
Your big blue pool-like eyes shine
Your face in complete symmetry, both sides the same
Your luscious lips, I wish to be mine

Your arms are a rippling mass
But, I, myself cannot have you
For beside you is a girl with class
The sight of you now makes me blue

I will always wish our love to be...
But as I look down the hall, I see a guy
His hair, too, is like the sun...oh, my love, goodbye!

Friends First

We were friends first
But then my heart began to burst
With emotions I never knew
I had for you

I admired you from afar
You were the center of my life, my star
Now you are gone
Like the moon at dawn

I love you more than ever
And will, always and forever

Friends Through Love

We became friends very quickly
Our friendship so very much like a rose
Beautiful, yet still prickly
And always appreciated by the nose

We got to know each other well
During which time I must admit
How much in love I fell
And how perfectly we fit

The disappointments kept coming my way
And love lost its glow
Such a conflict between what you do and say
It all seemed to make me low

Soon I spotted the mark of passion
That was burnt on your neck
Don't say it was your flirtatious fashion
Because it is my heart I must protect

Now I feel I must let you go
And be rid of such pain
Maybe find a charming new beau
Because the sun always shines after a rain

How Do I Tell You?

How do I tell you that I really love you?
How do I tell you that I really care?
How do I tell you that there's no one above you?
How do I tell you that I am always there?

Why doesn't the world just stop for us?
Why can't you just tell me you love me?
Is this one emotion worth all this fuss?
Or is there a hidden truth we cannot see?

My ears need to hear those words from you
Yet strangely, I don't really care
If they are I love you or Adieu
Even if one would be easier to bear

I Expected...

I expected...
a love you could not give.

I expected...
a life you could not live.

I expected...
words from your heart.

I expected...
that we would never part.

I expected...
some kind of devotion.

I expected...
a meaningful emotion.

I expected...
our lips to touch.

All in all...
I expected too much.

I Love You

I love you
Are the words my throat aches to utter

One touch of your hand
Makes my heart flutter

The thoughts of you near
Makes my body tense

My lips quiver
From suspense

My happiness will be
When we are one

Oh, for once let this
Horrible heartache be done

I See You

I see you and I know
That someday we will be

I see you and I know
That you don't see me

I see you and I know
That our love would be right

I see you and I know
That there is no future in sight

Love Letter

You started as a friend
But where, when did it end?

I think we can do better
So, I write you this letter

Not out of despair
But just because I care

It is you I love
More than the sky above

My heart pounds when you are near
So loud—you must hear

My sweet, sweet dreams at night
Of you pulling me in so tight

In my heart I have kept
The feelings you will never accept

Don't push me away
No matter what you say

Forever you will be
The only love for me

A Love Story

I'll tell you a story with no end
About a girl who fell in love with a friend

He was loving and caring in his own way
But he was attached, you could say

Yet still she kept her love in her heart
While secretly it was tearing her apart

She sat with her love unfound
She thought he was coming around

But he had no love for her
She was like a question but no answer

This has no happy ending
No quick-fix or easy mending

Just a girl who must pretend
Because she loved, loves, and will forever love her friend

My Path

Your glances leave me still
Your touches leave me warm
Your laughter lets me feel
When I watch you perform
You light a spark in me
That I thought had gone away
My path, I know will be
Beside you some near day

Only Love

Only love could hurt this way
tearing my heart day by day

Only love could feel so good
changing my appearance, changing my mood

Only love could be this complicated
make me love someone I should have hated

Only love could have the power
to grow or wilt such a lonely flower

Process of Love

I give my heart and soul to you
with every move I make
I leave you letters of my love
Hoping my heart won't break

I give up on this one-sided love
You become less and less to me
I look at my opportunities
And all the possibilities I see

But then you show your love
You miss me and you care
You let me forget the pain and betrayal
And I think I will fall again, if I dare

What Are You Doing with My Love?

What are you doing with my love?

I give it to you
but you don't take it

I say it to you
but you don't hear it

I show it to you
but you don't see it

What are you doing with my love?
It has turned my life upside down
And run me into the ground

What is left of me now?
I have to live on someway—somehow

What are you doing with my love?

When

When my heart began to race
I lost a part of me

When I fell in love with you
I lost a part of me

When we had our first fight
I lost a part of me

When I had to concede
I lost a part of me

When you disappointed my expectations
I lost a part of me

When I suffered in unrequited love
I lost a part of me

When I saw the first betrayal
I lost a part of me

When I tried to get away
I lost a part of me

When I feel like there is no more to lose
I lose that much more

I fear that I am too lost
Way down to my very core

Life & Other Observations

The world through the lens of a teenage girl.

The 5 Senses

I see a life full of light
I see a bird full of flight

I hear a man full of joy
I hear a box full of toys

I taste a dish full of care
I taste a drink full of air

I smell a tree full of pears
I smell a stable full of mares

I feel an ocean full of life
I feel a heart full of strife

Amanda McFadden

Adolescence

Your life is changing
The world is rearranging

Every move—unsure
Every thought—impure

Thinking you are all grown
But then you are thrown
By the mistakes you made
Regret cuts you like a blade

Your mistakes are plenty
But hindsight is twenty-twenty

Love is in the air
Blooming everywhere

Your heart breaks
But then something takes
The hurt away

But don't dare say
It is the "happiest of times"
Because that will end all rhymes

Alone

Alone
All by myself
Reserved
My own little place
No one to talk or listen to
I try to forget everything
Just sunny skies and green grass

There is a flash
Echoes surround me
Sad echoes, mad echoes
I search for happy echoes
The echoes stop

Sunny skies and green grass come again

A-R-T

Alluring to the soul
Like a man with a goal
With a heart as black as coal

Ready to burn the heart within
Feeding off the effect of sin
Mortal pain like the prick of a pin

Time only as an endless thought
Bringing together only what can be brought
Teaching only what cannot be taught

Alluring and Ready for Time

Bye, Friend

You take away my self-esteem
You never believe in me
You tell me I'm not a part of the team
My point of view, you refuse to see

You doubt my every word
What do I have to prove to you?
I am not one of a flock you herd
I am tired of feeling blue

I am me and that's enough
I am calling your bluff
I do not need your insight
So long, this is good night

Childhood

Tiny bulbs on a Christmas tree
used to bewilder me

Little boys at school
used to seem so cruel

A pig chasing a bunny
used to be so funny

Watching Sesame Street
used to be such a treat

A stranger who stared
used to leave me scared

Ideas sprang from bewilderment
Love sprang from hate
Humor sprang from delight
Insight sprang from innocence
Discernment sprang from fear

I've changed day by day
A little this way and that
Until a teenager sprang from a child

Friendship

The complex meeting of two opposite people
Sharing secrets, fears, and more
Supporting each other like a steeple
Creating the "friendship lunch" of lore
Fighting like foes
Making up like comrades
A loyalty as deep as it goes
Taking no more than it adds

I Watch

Through the midnight fire, I watch
Through the rising mill of heat, I watch
Through the changing leaves and growing trees, I watch
Through the fading tears and conquered fears, I watch
Unresolved and uninvolved, I watch

I watch as the wolves attack my friend—their prey
I watch the transformation of good to bad and love to hate
I watch the false hopes and broken promises they bring him

They take his heart; they take his soul
They destroy what they have stole
They think that no one sees their midnight fire
I watch and cry out, but I am called a liar
They have changed him as time wilts a flower
And willingly, he gave them the power

Keep It Coming

There sits a man in a bar on a stool
The windows are open, and the wind is cool
His problems this day are numerous
And his bartender, a tad too humorous

This man orders a whiskey—straight
He finishes his drink and starts to sedate
He asks the bartender to fill his glass
It's filled to the top and emptied in one pass

"Keep it coming," he says to the man behind the bar
The bartender is concerned if he will be driving a car
The man gets angry and demands another drink
Soon this man's eyelids begin to sink.

But he still wants another shot of the stuff
The barkeep lets him know he's had enough
The man throws his glass against the mirror on the wall
He takes out a gun and stands up straight and tall

The bartender and patrons scream in dread
The man tells them all to leave, or they will be dead
The bar is soon empty, except the man and the liquor
He pulls down all the shades and sits on a stool of wicker

He finds the bottle of whiskey, which he slowly sips
It's an hour before the last of it passes his lips
The next morning, he is found without life
Surrounded by jugs of whiskey, a day after the death of his wife

My Dream

I see this dream
This dream of mine
In colors that beam
In one straight line

I see my goal
An endless hope
Escape from my soul
But no linking rope

And that which holds
The ultimate conclusion
That my life molds
With a careful illusion

My eyes do not rest
On every tiny detail
Not yet expressed
And ever so frail

Those that show
No rough angles
And still, I know
The truth dangles

It's in front of me
Seeming so near
That it must be
Something sincere

Life

Encircled by enduring emotions
Embraced by everlasting love
Full as a contented man's belly
Empty as unfilled promises
As united as a circle
As broken as a young lover's heart
Beginning in a moment
Ending in a second

Prey

The bird up in a tree
Spreading its wings to fly
Never thinks he won't see
Land under him whiz by

While at the same time a bear
Sleeping in a cave so snug
May not even be aware
That he will soon be a rug

What about that little rabbit
Happily hopping in the meadow
Will it know to be still and sit
Before it too must go?

The Ramble of the Insane

Images swirl around my mind
Each one different than the other
None of the same kind
Their colors could smother
Even the most romantic of poets
There is only one common denominator
Which is in front of me, and I know it
But I deny the meaning to cater
To the whims of my constitution
My mind rambles on as such
That no query or investigation
Could shed light on or touch
My exact intent in this thinking
Soon though my mind becomes clear
And irrational ideals start shrinking
Until all that is left is my sense of fear

Reflection

I see the person I never was
Through the mistakes I have made
Days forgotten just because
The memories seem to fade

Remembering people from my past
By conversations lost in time
Decisions made too fast
Because I could do no crime

Never knowing what I have done
Never knowing what I lost that day
Friendship is a loaded gun
Whose bullets I let ricochet

Relationships

The word itself, so complicated
And pertaining to friends, lovers, and those related
The proper meaning being to relate
Yet its value is still a great debate

One might summarize such a state
As a glimpse into the soul of your mate
The hours and days which you must dedicate
To calm the quarrels that you may instigate

Drawing a line that is not straight
We cross this line to investigate
The mystical wonder that cannot wait

Two people brought together by fate
May "relate" just a little too late
And as I have previously stated
The word itself is so complicated

The Sad Good Girl

A good girl is what I am
I don't do drugs, smoke, or drink
I should be a happy little lamb
But I feel like a ship about to sink
My friends say, try it, do it
I say no
Now they are excluding me bit by bit
Oh sure, they put on quite a show
But "no" is what it will forever be
I'd rather be without friends
Then let peer pressure take hold of me

Summer Rains

Small drops of water hit the ground
Each making their own individual sound
Soon they build a miniature lake
Perfect circles they make

The smell of damp air
Getting wet without a care
Dreaming my dreams
Knowing nothing is what it seems

My waterfall wonder stops
Sensibility clears my head of raindrops

There Was a Time

There was a time not long ago
When life was but a gloomy day
The world seemed motionless and slow
Giving off only shades of gray

I chose my path with an open soul
Which gives me some justification
Until it finally took its toll
And the truth was suffocating

Time had passed a lot faster than I thought
Peace had to be met before the end came
Emotions had to be caressed not bought
Not to say that life would remain the same

Time

I see it come towards me
It comes fast and then leaves
How can I stop it?
I grab hold but it slips
My hands are not strong enough
I want it to stay with me
I invite it
I beg it
It leaves

We Were Friends

We were friends
For oh, so long
Fights come and it ends
Something always goes wrong

So much wasted time
Too many things said
Hearing clocks chime
Away our life until we're dead

What are we today?
Why are we doing this?
I have got something to say:
It is you I miss

We Will Go Away

Soon the day will arrive
that we anxiously await
Soon we will leave this school
that we like to say we hate

Soon we will wear tassels
and little square hats
Soon we will hug and cry
and share reassuring pats

Soon we will walk up the steps
and across the big stage
Soon we will hold a diploma
that will yellow with age

Soon we will go to a college
or university someplace
Soon we will get impressive jobs
and have more problems to face

Soon we will get married
to the one that we cherish
Soon we will go away
But our memories will never perish

Why, Oh Why

The world is dreary
My heart is weary
Why, oh why?

Everywhere is gloom
Life is an imminent doom
Why, oh why?

Time is sadness
Violence is madness
Why, oh why?

Love is depressing
Living is suppressing
Why, oh why?

Words Don't Rhyme

My poems don't rhyme anymore
My thoughts don't flow with ink
My words don't come together
My ability is gone

Why?
How can I answer?

The turns of life have crushed me
I can't flow
I can't write
I can't express the way I feel
Everything has stopped
Including this feeble attempt to write

Now...

9:22

Isn't it sad that crying,
Well, it rhymes with dying.
No lies that I am lying,
But I am not flying.

My self-conceived dream of blue
That's lacking without you.
Are you the dream I once knew,
At dark 9:22?

Questions flood past like red wine
And everything seems fine.
What an anamorphic line
In my life of the brine.

Blanc

A blank canvas is like
An unpainted concoction
That's utterly ignored, psych,
And sold at an auction
To a buyer far away
In a country too rich
Unknown to its castaway
To one day in a ditch.

Blows

Fast paced; two moments.
Fire. Blow.
Unreal atonements.
Parry. Go.
Fine artwork; convenience.
Worry. No.
Your lone; obedience.
Wary. Show.
Obstructed media.
Kicking. Woah.
Encyclopedia.
Breathing. Low.
The dumb die and some live.
Grieving. Oh.
The dumb lie and some give.
Leaving. Foe.

The Crowd

Away
Away in a crowd
A crowd that's loud
A crowd that vowed

To never love
The gentle dove
From above
That they shove

Your worries
Your hurries
You're every doubt
And roundabout.

Quiet
That's the way
You should play
Don't ever say

Your ever doubt
Your never bout
With death itself
The breath you shelf

On a corner
You never walk by
Until one day
You die.

The Door and the Fan

Is it fair that I cry
On a bench all alone,
Where the good men will die
On their self-imposed throne?

Is it right that I walk
While others are not free
In a country of chalk,
Where the free cannot be?

Is it weird that I stay,
Yet I cannot remain
In the safety I stray
And will never attain?

Is it strange that I can
Free myself from a trap
Of the door and the fan
That's open in my lap?

Forested

In that mire,
On that day.
Where I find
I will stay.
Will you come?
Will you slay?
Will myself
Be the ray?

Where I fled,
Where I flee.
I will cry
On a knee
That's not there
Or will be
On a ground
I can't see.

Why you left
I don't know.
Is because
I can't show
Pain of life
That won't go.
Hurt you bad,
And I woe.

Still I love,
Still I hate.
That you left
With your date.
Without you,
I relate.
There is death,
There is fate.

Trent McFadden

Goodbye, Childhood.

Sometimes I look at me
And what do I see?
A crying face staring
Red-eyed and daring.
Where did childhood go?
I can never know.
Because life rips your soul
The net and the goal.

Graves Are Like Reality

There are some things that should not be said
And words are like a book
There are some things that should not be read
And books are like a king
There are some things that should not be led
And kings are like a grave
There are some things that should not be dead
And graves are like reality

Trent McFadden

I Fear the World

I fear the world,
And that's not wrong
Or even mad
Since it's a song
We often sing
On nights so long,
Where it's noisy,
A noisy gong.

It's Back

Some,
Some unwitting moment
You open
You read
The past.
Soon,
Far too soon
You realize
And regret
Too fast.

So,
It floods
It shakes
Ultimately breaks
Your mind.
Breath,
Close
Your eyes
And find.

The dust.
The age-old.
The page-gold
Foretold
Stories of you.
But from a time
An age,
A life
So distant
From who?

The tears.
They fly

Like the pages
The sages
Of a different realm.
You, you cannot recognize
Yourself
Oh, ago
At the helm.

Before,
Before your lies
Demise
Ties
Your night.
Might as well,
Be old
Millions
Of years
You fight.

Where,
Where did it go
And stay
To haunt you
The ghoul.
Somewhere,
The answer.
The killer.
The robber.
The tool.

It's Been a Pleasure

Have we sought past
The life that we fast?
Or give away,
Just like yesterday?

I'll never know
For too much I show
To the world grind
In heart and in mind.

It's Gone

There comes a day,
Sooner than expected.
Where the palm trees sway,
And crash down, rejected.

Where beaches don't glow
And the sunset fades.
No longer you know
Your childhood glades.

The Lilies, in Summer

In the summer day
The lilies dance.
All around they play
The name is Chance.

But a shadow looms
And stomps it out.
Leather boot that dooms
The name is Doubt.

A forgotten husk
Lies on that lawn.
The sun becomes dusk
The name is Gone.

Trent McFadden

The Mirror's Man

He.
He feels fabulous in the mirror.
Even though.
Even though he's far from pure.
Sleeping.
Sleeping in the dark.
Killing.
Killing like a shark.

Morbid Comforts

I like it when
The pages brush past.
Because it's then
I can kill my cast.

I like it when
The dark feels alone.
Because it's then
I can truly hone.

I like it when
The tears fall like rain.
Because it's then
I can feel my pain.

Trent McFadden

My Shell

I die.
I die in the mind.
I die in the grind.
I die in what I find.
In you.
It's true
That angels cry
And angels die
Like you.
I never knew
What life could be
And I never see
Past doubt.
My route
In a shell.
Where I fell.
And I cry.
And I die.
Why do I cry?
Why do I die?

I'll never know in this shell.

The Mystery of All Time

Time is like a rose in bloom.
For a while it catches your eye.
But as all roses meet their doom,
So will time eventually die.

Time is like grains of sand.
It fills the beachy coast.
But as you grasp it in the hand,
It vanishes instantly, almost.

Night

Sleep evades yet fades
Into my mind.
I halt,
For what I find
Is gone
A thought so dear.
A song
No one will hear.

None of Us, That's Who

I tried once
On a fretted night
To find one
Just one human right
A perfect
Not flawed human soul
A human
Who makes righteousness their goal.

Curse that night
I should have never even tried
For humans
Every last one sinned and died
So like you
Seeker of wisdom that's true
So like me
A soul to endlessly rue.

Of the Coward

Who is the Coward?
He is but a man,
A pitiful can
In the soup of life.
What harm is the Coward?
For he fears it all,
The door and the fall
Of the place of strife.

Why hate the Coward?
For essence of fear,
Is more than a tear
We risk to suffer.
Are you the Coward?
Fleeing from hate,
Hopelessly irate
To make us rougher.

On My Mind

The night cold enveloped me,
But I felt no chill.
The icy winds surrounded me,
But I felt so still.

I had just survived the worst,
A damaging fray.
I had been a brave soldier,
A man who will stay.

The wound was bloody and deep,
Yet I felt no stain.
The wound should have been fatal,
Yet I felt no pain.

The blood flowed red like crimson,
And yet I push on.
The blood ran cold and dreary,
And yet the flow's gone.

Safety is my only goal,
With nothing else there.
Safety is hope for my wound,
With red skin so bare.
Nothing else is on my mind,
As wounds are for the dead.
Nothing else will capture me,
As blood is only red.

The Other Bear

You could be a critic
And I wouldn't care
Or would I do
Because I'm a bear
Looking for views
So I despair
Over mindless drivel
I always share.

Pitiful Love

Like catching the wind with hands
Or eating with rubber bands
Is like trying to talk
Or even walk
To the one you love.

Rash Bear

It fell apart like a flash
Because you,
Just you,
Became rash.

And now, you want to cry
Cry inside
And cry
to die.

But,
You can't care
Because no one
Can dare.

To love
The crying child,
Who's not tender,
nor mild.

And can't
Live up quite yet
Not while
His tears set.

So you
Did another sin
Rash blunder, blunder
That you win.

Like a holler,
Like a ring
Like a child
That can't cling.

To a life
That feels unfair
Because no one
Can ever dare.

And you,
You can't beware
Your inner rash,
Rash bear.

The Return

On a whistle, on an ember
On a night in December
The lies I remember
Come back to dismember

My bones, my life
My endless, ever strife
My vice, where it's rife
The habit, the knife.

See the Lilies

See, see the lilies
See the lilies before they pass away
Float away
Fly away
To come back no other day

Because,
One, one fateful day
They'll fold
And mold
Become fool's, fool's fake gold
Become the essence
Of the nightmares you were told.

Young,
Innocent and blind,
Remember.
Remember in your mind.
The lilies.
The lilies that you find.
The lilies.
Before away they grind.

Shredded Story

At the moment,
At the moment,
Doesn't it feel bare?
Pointless.
Empty
Pointless to share.

A burden to society.
A burden
To loath.
A failure,
Ashamed.
Ashamed that you dove.

Because,
Because it's terrible
And you miss it.
Rubbish.
Castaway.
Or is it?

Smeared Ink

Smeared.
On the window
Of your life.
On the distance
From your wife.
And yet you will never strife.

Geared.
To be distant
From the way.
To be distant
From today.
And yet you give it away.

Feared.
As a travel
To inside.
As a gravel
You confide.
And yet you can never hide.

Something I Had

Was it late that night?
Was it a clock read?
For I feel I might
Finally fall dead.

Was it yes, or no?
Was it good, or bad?
Was something I know
Something I had?

Sometimes. But Only Sometimes.

Sometimes
I feel like
The world hates
Me.
And what fates
Me.
Is naught

Sometimes
I feel like
Crying
And
Dying.
And die crying
In your arms.

To Cry

Break.
It takes more than love to
Hate.
My soul you shove
And wait.
For my only love
To fate.
My restless dove.

Cry.
Inside and worry
High.
In mind and body,
But lie.
Forever to wary.
Who die.
Like all the merry,
Cry.

To My Soul of Me

These lines I see,
These vines I be.
To my soul of me,
Those wines of she.

These dots I see,
These thoughts I be.
To my soul of me,
Those lots of she.

These days I see,
These ways I be.
To my soul of me,
Those rays of she.

These fights I see,
These nights I be.
To my soul of me,
Those sights of she.

These dies I see,
These cries I be.
To my soul of me,
Those lies of she.

Wander

Some voices like to wander.
Wander where you hide,
Find where you reside.
They are what you confide.

Some people like to wander
Wander where you talk,
Burn where you walk.
They are what you will mock.

Some inane like to wander.
Wander where you stay,
Follow you today.
They are what you relay.

Some lepers like to wander.
Wander where you know,
Follow you on though.
They are what you will throw.

And What is a Man?

Can you truly run?
I think I'm done
With the life you gun,
And what is fun?

I just want to live
And not to give
My own life away
So I can play.

I find you and me,
Just pointlessly
At odds of the sea
Without the glee.

To the place I ran
And with the fan
Of consistency
All over me.

The life that I had
So yet so sad
One time like a fad
That's gone and bad.

Trent McFadden

Wonder on a Cold Morning

Maybe you're someone
Who's a bit like me
Standing on the corner
Of insanity
Life in confinement
On the great white sea
Long in desperation
To be truly free

Your Tears

Do you see those tears?
Those are your tears, not mine.

They can't dry.
They can't die.
They can't fly.

But they can cry.

And this what they will do
Until someday,
Someday,
They'll find you.

About the Authors

Amanda McFadden lives in the California Central Valley with her husband and 3 children. She works remotely solving technical support issues every day! In her spare time, she makes lists of what she should be doing.

Trent McFadden lives in the California Central Valley with his mom, dad, sister, and brother. He attends an online high school and is getting a jump start on college through a local community college. In his spare time, he writes short stories and poetry and creates pixel art.